THE SPACE SHIP UNDER THE APPLE TREE

LOUIS SLOBODKIN

The Space Ship Under the Apple Tree

COLLIER BOOKS New York, New York
COLLIER-MACMILLAN LTD., LONDON

The Macmillan Company, 866 Third Avenue,
New York, N.Y. 10022
Collier-Macmillan Canada Ltd., Toronto, Ontario

First Collier Books Edition 1971
The Space Ship Under the Apple Tree is also published in a hardcover edition by The Macmillan Company.

Printed in the United States of America

CONTENTS

1. FALLING STARS

One night in mid-August just before he went to bed, Eddie Blow stood on his grandmother's porch looking up at the star-filled sky.

"There's a lot of shooting stars out tonight, Grandma," he said. "Come on out and look. . . . There's lots of them."

"Make a wish, Eddie," called his grandmother from the kitchen.

"What's that, Grandma?"

"Make a wish, Eddie," she repeated. "That's what you should do when you see a falling star."

"Aw, Grandma," said Eddie. "That's superstit—superstition. I mean . . . wishing on falling stars. Falling stars are meteors. Chunks of matter that are flung off—off into space and things. . . ."

"Wait a minute, Eddie. I can't hear a thing," called his grandmother. She had turned on a water tap in the kitchen. "Wait just a minute, son. I'll be with you in a minute and then you can tell me."

In a little while she came out the door, wiping her hands on her apron. "Now what were you saying, Eddie?"

"I was just saying, Grandma. Wishing on falling stars is— Well, falling stars are great meteors or something. They shoot off like that, burning all the time. Sometimes they don't burn out altogether and they fall to earth . . . and make big holes. . . . Look, there's one! There's a beauty! . . . It just went over the ridge back of the apple orchard!"

"My! My!" said his grandmother. "That was a beauty. But I surely wish that it did go over the ridge and did not come down to earth. It would have come down just about on top of Grandfather's apple tree. If I were to make a wish on *that* star, I'd just wish it didn't come down on Grandfather's apple tree and break it up."

Grandfather's apple tree was the oldest tree in the orchard. It was called Grandfather's apple tree because it was said to be the first tree planted by Eddie's grandmother's grandfather. And all the trees in the orchard were said to be the children, grandchildren and great-grandchildren of Grandfather's apple tree.

"I guess it didn't. But I wish one of them would come down around here somewhere," said Eddie, and he hastily added, "just a little one, Grandma, one that wouldn't hurt anything. It wouldn't hurt anything if it came down, maybe, in the road."

"Well, none of them will be coming down just by wishing them down," said his grandmother. "And it's getting late anyway, Eddie boy. You'd better get off to bed. I just wish if that big star or meteor or whatever it was did come down, it hasn't come down on Grandfather's tree and broken it all up. Eddie, you'd better get off to bed. I'd like to have you go up to the orchard the first thing tomorrow morning. I'm just a little bit worried about Grandfather's apple tree."

"O.K., Grandma. 'Course I'll go up to the orchard," said Eddie. "Don't worry about that old meteor. Bet it's just whirling off into space right this minute. G'night, Grandma."

Eddie went up the stairs two at a time, swung the door of his room as if he'd tear the door off its hinges, took a running jump and plunked onto his bed. Then he ripped off one of his shoes without undoing the laces and stopped . . . and thought . . . .

What if the meteor really did come down in the apple orchard?

What if it did come down on Grandfather's apple tree?

What if it were up there right now, burning and burning?

What did it look like, burning away like that?

Eddie Blow was an eleven-and-a-half-year-old boy, who wore glasses and was interested in science and nature. He often stopped and asked himself questions about things and then tried to find out. In New York, where he lived all fall, winter and spring, Eddie read a lot of books in the library about science and nature. And his Boy Scout troop often went to the Natural History Museum. There Eddie found out about lots of things.

The small apartment where he lived with his mother in New York was rather crowded with his own collection of animals. He had a rabbit, a turtle, two white mice, a horned toad, a salamander, a family of guppies, a few goldfish and an assortment of spiders, moths and some other insects in a cardboard box. He also owned a ninth part of an absent-minded carrier pigeon named Bixxy.

The other eight parts of Bixxy were owned by eight other boys, who with Eddie had found and taken care of Bixxy some time ago when all nine boys were members of a Cub Scout den. Bixxy had been an Army pigeon and was somewhat of a hero.

Besides his collection of living animals, Eddie had a collection of arrowheads, coins, pieces of stones, shells, cocoons, birds' eggs, pressed flowers, leaves and ferns and a lot of other things. Every summer, when his mother sent him up the Hudson River to visit his grandmother at her farm, a few miles above Albany, she warned him.

"Eddie," she'd say, "I'll try to take care of

your collection while you're gone, but if I can't, I can't. . . . So don't be surprised . . . ."

But Eddie was never surprised. He always came home to find the animals in his collection as healthy as ever and often a lot cleaner, because of his mother's care, than they usually were.

At his grandmother's farm Eddie had no collection of animals. He did not need any, for he was able to see the birds, animals and insects living in their natural habitat. The farm sprawled up over the side of a steep hill. It was a big farm, but the soil was too stony to raise any crops of corn or wheat or things like that, though it did have a large apple orchard. And in the early spring Eddie's grandmother hired men to spray the apple trees. In the fall she again hired the men to pick, pack and cart away the big red apples. But during the long summer months Eddie was the only man who worked on her farm (so she said).

Eddie helped around the farm as much as possible, went to the village on errands and almost always did anything he was asked to do. His first job tomorrow morning was to go up to the apple orchard for Grandma, he told himself, as he slowly took off his other shoe.

"But why wait till morning?" he asked himself suddenly. "If that old meteor landed, it's burning right now, I bet. . . . Maybe I ought to go up tonight. . . ."

He heard his grandmother's bedroom door close.

Eddie thought another moment or two. Then he quietly got his flashlight and slipped out of his bedroom window. As lithe as a cat, he slid down the water drainpipe and landed on the ground below with a gentle thud.

The moon had risen and the road up the hill to the orchard was well lit. Little animals scurried across Eddie's path as he walked quickly along the road. He scrambled over the stone wall that separated the orchard from the road and then went on up through the orchard. The moon threw shadows of the leaves and branches on the orchard floor. The whole ground looked as if it were covered with a beautiful patterned rug.

When Eddie rounded the fat trunk of one of the sturdy children of Grandfather's apple tree he got his first clear view of the old tree.

At first glance there seemed nothing unusual. Grandfather's apple tree stood out clearly against the rising moon. There was no sign of any fallen meteors or anything else strange about the old apple tree.

Then Eddie saw something that made the hairs on the back of his neck stand up straight!

On a stout branch of the old tree, about ten feet up from the ground, something moved! It had looked like part of the tree, a leafless, strangely shaped, small branch attached to the stout branch. . . . Then it moved! It was the figure of a little man!

The little man was standing on the branch. But he was not standing on the top side of it. He stood on the bottom side of it! Head down! And he stood there as naturally as if his feet were firmly planted on the broad flat ground!

The little man was about three feet tall. He seemed to be looking out over the moonlit countryside with a tiny spyglass. Suddenly the little man fell like a shot, head first from the branch! He landed with a bang on his head. But his fall had no effect on him at all, for he was up on his feet in an instant. As he stood up he saw Eddie for the first time.

"Speak . . . English?" he asked in a high-pitched voice.

"Y-e-s, . . . sir," stammered Eddie.

"Good," said the little man. "One moment. . . . Must adjust non-gravity shoes."

The little man crouched on the ground, twirled some knobs on the heavy soles of the shoes he wore. Then he stood up and walked over to the trunk of Grandfather's apple tree and he kept right on walking, straight up the side of the tree and back along the big branch he had been clinging to (head down) when Eddie first saw him!

"One minute," said the little man again. "Must record observations."

After a minute or two of peeking through his little spyglass, he took what seemed to be a tiny typewriter out of one of his pockets. He quickly tapped its keys a number of times. Then he slipped it back into his pocket and marched back along the tree branch. He walked down the tree trunk to the ground and right up to the astounded Eddie!

"You . . . are native," he said.

"What?" exclaimed Eddie.

"One minute," said the little man. He pulled a little box out of another of the many pockets in his short jacket. He snapped it open. The box seemed filled with luminous little cards. He squinted at one of the cards and then he spoke again.

"You . . . are . . . born in United States . . . of America?"

"Yes, sir," said Eddie.

"Good," said the little man. "One minute."

The little man consulted his little luminous box again. As he squinted through some of the little cards Eddie began to get over the first shock of seeing the little man. "What's going on here?" he said to himself. "Who is he to ask me a lot of questions in my grandmother's apple orchard?"

"Look here!" said Eddie in a loud, angry voice. "What's going on here? Who are you? Who do you think you are, asking me a lot of questions in my own grandmother's apple orchard. You'd better . . . ."

As Eddie talked, the little man stopped looking through his luminous box. He adjusted a small knob on a bracelet he wore on his wrist. And as Eddie's voice rose angrily the little man suddenly touched Eddie's chest lightly with one of his fingers.

Eddie sat down hard on the ground!

"Speak slow. . . . No anger," said the little man.

Eddie scrambled to his feet, his fists clenched.

The little man held out his finger menacingly.

Eddie stood breathing hard.

"I answer question," said the little man. "I Scientist Explorer from Planet Martinea."

Eddie gasped. Then as he remembered his reading in astronomy books, he said doubtfully, "Martinea? The planet Martinea? G'wan, there's no such planet!"

The little man hastily consulted his little box again and ruffled through its luminous pages.

"What means g'wan?" he asked.

"G'wan means . . . . What difference does it make?" asked Eddie. "What's that box?"

"This box explains language. English language, Martinean language," said the man. "Dictionary Box. Our Language Scientists study American English through high-powered telescopes from Martinea."

"How could they?" asked Eddie suspiciously.

"Your language on highways— 'Go slow!

Speed limit forty miles! Turn left! Hot Dogs! Welcome to Hoosic Falls!' Our Language Scientists construct language from these examples."

Eddie just blinked.

"Where's this Martinea?" he asked.

The little man pointed in the general direction beyond the moon.

"Martinea outside your sun's orbit," said the little man.

"Yeah? Well, I never heard of it," said Eddie.

"What is yeah?" asked the little man, quickly consulting his dictionary box again.

"Never mind that," said Eddie. "If you did come from this Martinea, how'd you get here?"

The little man looked at Eddie as if he were making up his mind, then he spoke again.

"Come, I show you."

And he turned and walked over the ridge in back of Grandfather's apple tree. Eddie followed. About ten feet from the tree trunk, the little man stopped, then quickly and with surprising strength he began to pull away a lot of old branches that filled a rather large gully.

Eddie didn't remember ever seeing that gully before.

In a few minutes the gully was cleared. The moonlight revealed a metal something which looked very much like an immense over-turned metal dish. It was about fifteen feet in diameter. There were strange gadgets on its metal surface and along the outer rim, regularly placed, were a number of small metal tubes.

"A flying saucer!" exclaimed Eddie. "Say, that looks like . . . . No, it can't be, it's impossible! There are no such things as flying saucers!"

The little man turned to Eddie, then he quickly snapped open his little dictionary box again. "F . . . f . . . frying pan? Flying . . . ," he muttered as he flipped through the cards in the box. "There are no flying saucers. What is flying saucers?"

"Sure," said Eddie. "There are no flying saucers. I read it in a scientific magazine in the library, *The World Scientist*. A big professor, what's his name, Professor Something said there are no such things as flying saucers."

"What is name of scientific magazine?"

asked the little man, "*World Scientist?* Professor Something?"

The little man had taken out his little typewriter again and tapped away at it for a second.

"This, Astral Rocket Disk, perhaps you say space ship," he said. And as he spoke he began to cover his space ship again, "Professor Something correct. . . . No flying saucers!"

When he had finished covering the space ship the little man turned to Eddie.

"Information please," he said. "Where hotel? Must rest. Must wait for . . . how you say, this side earth revolve to sun?"

"You mean until daylight," said Eddie.

"Yes, daylight," said the little man.

"There's no hotel around here," said Eddie, "only farms. If you want to rest tonight. . . . Tell you what, come down to my grandmother's house. It's down there." Eddie pointed in the direction of his grandmother's house. "You can rest tonight. She won't mind. . . . I think. I got a chest in my room long enough for you."

"Good," said the little man. "Speed limit forty miles."

He adjusted some knobs on his large shoes,

set a little dial in the direction Eddie had pointed and took off. Eddie found himself racing down through the orchard after the little man, who moved with amazing speed toward Eddie's grandmother's house.

2. THE LITTLE MAN

Eddie wasn't sure whether it was the sun streaming into his window or his grandmother's voice which woke him the next morning. As he lay there half awake, he said to himself, "Dreams are good things. A fellow can have more adventure with his eyes closed than he can when they're wide open. Dream about flying . . . dream about falling . . . dream . . . ."

Eddie yawned, stretched and closed his eyes again.

"Be down in a minute, Grandma," he

mumbled sleepily as he dug his head back into the pillow.

After a minute or two his grandmother called up from the kitchen again.

"Eddie, . . . Remember what you promised. . . . Remember you said you would go up to the orchard for me."

Eddie's eyes flashed open. That's what he had dreamed about, going up to the orchard! Or did he dream it? Eddie sat bolt upright in his bed as he remembered the little man He jerked his head around and looked over at the chest where the little man had stretched out after they climbed up the drainpipe to Eddie's room.

There was no one on the chest!

Quickly Eddie looked around his room. There was no sign of the little man.

"Whew!" said Eddie, sinking back on his pillow with a sigh of relief. "What a dream that was!"

"Ed-die. . . . Are you getting up?" called his grandmother from the foot of the stairs.

"Coming, Grandma," shouted Eddie and he popped out of bed, dressed himself and was down the stairs in a jiffy.

"My, Eddie!" cried his grandmother as he rushed into the kitchen. "That's the quickest I ever saw you wake up. Like a regular five-alarm fire."

Eddie grinned over the edge of a large glass of orange juice and said nothing. His grandmother had to tell him again and again during the rest of his breakfast to slow up and chew before he swallowed.

The moment Eddie could, he raced out of the house.

"S'long, Grandma," he said as he swung out the door. "I'm going up to the orchard to look at Grandfather's apple tree."

"Please let me know soon," cried his grandmother after him. "Don't go off anywhere until you've told me."

"I won't," shouted Eddie over his shoulder as he ran up the road. He ran hard over the flat stretches and dog-trotted up the hilly sections until he climbed up the orchard to Grandfather's apple tree.

He arrived out of breath at the top of the ridge. There was nothing unusual about the big spreading apple tree. Some birds twittered here and there, a chipmunk took off into space, some fruit flies whirled around some invisible something in mid-air. Aside from the buzzing of the flies, the twittering of the birds and the rat-tat-tat of a hidden woodpecker nearby, there was no other sign or sound of life around the big tree.

Eddie held his breath as he circled the gnarled trunk of the tree. He looked down toward the mysterious gully he had seen, or dreamed about, during the night. There was no sign of the gully; the ground looked solid and was covered with twigs, leaves and moss. The rat-tat-tat sound of the hidden woodpecker grew louder. Just as Eddie was about to say to himself, "Slush, there's no such gully," up from what seemed to be solid earth popped a little figure. It was the little man again! In his hand he held a small bright instrument. It was about the shape and size of a dentist's drill.

"Come here," said the little man.

Eddie approached cautiously. As he came closer, the little man suddenly called out sharply like a train conductor, "Watch step!"

Eddie stopped short and not a moment too soon, for he saw now that the mysterious gully really did exist. At that moment he stood at the edge of it. The seemingly solid ground was just a mass of great branches, twigs, leaves and moss, so cleverly arranged that from a few feet away the gully was completely disguised.

The little man stood waist deep in the center of the gully. Suddenly he ducked down into the hole and was up in an instant. Now he held something that looked like a metal pinwheel.

"One minute," said the little man.

He touched a button on the handle of the pinwheel. The wheel began to whir. The little man watched it carefully, and when his pinwheel was whirring so fast the little blades had run together into a transparent, silver disk, he held it at arm's length above his head.

In an instant the little man was pulled up into space, then zi-p he'd hopped to the rim of the gully and stood alongside Eddie. "Radiomatic Heliocopter Miniature," he explained, pointing to his little pinwheel.

"Oh!" said Eddie after he had swallowed the lump of surprise that rose in his throat.

The little man seemed a lot friendlier than he had been last night, Eddie thought.

"You inspect Astral Rocket Disk?" he asked.

Eddie started to nod his head. But before

his chin had reached his neck, the little man had a firm grip on Eddie's arm, and he found himself flying through the air. In a flash they were over the hole at the center of the gully. The little man gently let Eddie down through the hole.

"Walk down," said the little man as he hovered over Eddie's head.

Eddie carefully stepped down. He found he had climbed down into the hidden Astral Rocket Disk!

3. THE ASTRAL ROCKET DISK

Eddie climbed down a small ladder and he now stood in a circular room inside the space ship. The room was well lighted, but Eddie could not see the source of the light. There were no bulbs or lamps. The strange, blue-tinged light seemed to come directly from the walls. There were no shadows in the circular room. It was about ten feet in diameter and about six feet high. There was a fat metal column, which extended from the floor to the ceiling in the center of the room. Various gadgets, wheels, levers and gauges covered one-half of the room. The other half was simply furnished with cabinets, and there was a line of small rings and knobs attached to the ceiling over the cabinets.

The little man, who had followed Eddie down the ladder, proudly pointed out and named the equipment in the Astral Rocket Disk.

"This Supersonic Denotator, Electronic Amplifier, Hypersensitive Pacifier, Micro-Photometer, Spectrometer, Monochrometer, Inter-Angilated Eliminator, Cospacial Larinator, Interspacial Communication System, Adrio-Dynamic Desensitizer . . . ."

When he could not think of the proper English word for the gadget he was pointing to, he would consult his little dictionary box. Sometimes even the box failed him, since some of the names of the instruments could not be translated. Then the little man used his own language. It sounded like Welsh, or what Eddie thought Welsh might sound like if he ever heard it.

"Here is Willewingulagulin," said the little man, pointing to a very small crystal-covered gadget. "Not good. Not used on modern Astral Rocket Disks. This old space ship."

"How old?" asked Eddie, glad to change

the subject because he was getting a little dizzy from the long list of scientific words.

The little man consulted his luminous box.

"One-half earth revolution around your sun."

Eddie figured fast.

"Why, that's a half year, six months," said Eddie. "It sure looks brand-new."

"This equipment old now. Modern Martinean Astral Rocket Disks very different," said the little man with a touch of pride in his voice.

"Things must get old fast in Martinea," said Eddie.

"Time different in Martinea," said the little man. "We use light years. How old you your time?"

"I'm eleven going on twelve," said Eddie, and since the little man looked doubtful he explained, "Guess you'd say eleven complete earth revolutions around our sun, and a half revolution."

The little man frowned, then he walked over to the cabinet side of the room; there he reached over his head and pulled a small ring. A blackboard unrolled, like a window shade, from the ceiling and stiffened. The little man snapped out his little box, looked into it and then turned to Eddie.

"Eleven and one-half revolutions . . . years?" he asked.

"Yeah," said Eddie. "Eleven and a half years. That's right. Eleven and a half revolutions."

The little man turned back to the blackboard; for the next few minutes he scribbled curious little marks on the board with a luminous chalk. He worked furiously for a while. He seemed to be adding, subtracting, multiplying, dividing (long division and short), doing fractions and square roots. Soon he had the board covered with thousands of little luminous marks, checks, stars, dots and arrows. Finally, all his arithmetic was reduced at the very bottom of the blackboard to just three little marks.

He turned to Eddie with a surprised expression on his face. He pointed to the little marks, then to himself and then to Eddie.

"You—I, same old! I eleven and a half years," he said. "Eleven and half earth revolutions around your sun."

"Say, you're smart!" exclaimed Eddie in admiration.

"Smart?" said the little man as he reached for his little box again. But he changed his mind, because even though he did not know what "smart" meant it was obvious Eddie meant something nice.

"Lookit, since you and I are the same age," said Eddie enthusiastically, "let's you and I be friends. What d'you say? Let's be friends, huh?"

"Friends?" asked the little man. "Friends?"

Eddie groaned under his breath as the little man dug into his little box again.

"F . . . F . . . Foals . . . Fools . . . Furniture . . . F . . . F . . . . No friends," said the little man. "No word 'friends' in my language. What is 'friends'?"

"Well, friends is . . . ," began Eddie, "when two fellows . . . . Oh, friends is . . . , you know, like . . . ."

And Eddie was embarrassed. It was so hard to explain what anyone means by "friends" to someone who had no such word in his language. After a few minutes of stumbling around Eddie gave up.

"All right," he said, "let's not be friends."

"Inspect Astral Rocket Disk more?" suggested the little man after a moment of silence.

"Yes, thanks," said Eddie. "How does it work?"

The little man motioned to the cabinet side of the room. He pulled another small ring, which hung from the ceiling, and unrolled a sheet of what looked like beautifully translucent glass. The sheet of pliable glass, hanging from the ceiling, stiffened and was as rigid as the blackboard.

"Interior - Exterior - Radar - Intercommunicator," said the little man.

"What's it for?" asked Eddie.

"Watch," said the little man. He twisted the little ring and the sheet of glass began to cloud. Then it cleared again. And Eddie found himself looking into a very sharp reflection of the room where they stood in the space ship. But it was not a mirror reflection. There were two figures in the room. One he recognized as the back view of the little man. The other someone (a little taller someone) was wearing blue jeans. . . . Why, it was a back view of himself, Eddie! He had never noticed his own ears before, and since he could, he wiggled his right ear. The figure of himself in the glass wiggled his right ear, too. Yes, sir, that was him, Eddie.

"This interior of Astral Rocket Disk," announced the little man. "Now here exterior of Astral Rocket Disk," and he switched the little ring at the bottom of the glass screen again. Instantly the glass clouded and cleared again. Eddie found himself looking at the outside of the Astral Rocket Disk. It did look like two large metal dishes stuck together with a line of small tubes around the rim.

"Boy, that's neat," said Eddie. "How does the disk work? How does it fly, I mean?"

"Tubes on rim are rockets," said the little man. "Revolve at great speed. See cross section." And the little man whirled the ring again.

Now Eddie saw the picture on the glass as if the Astral Rocket Disk were cut in half. He could see the little man and himself inside. And he could see that the wall of the room they stood in was entirely separated from the outside wall of the Astral Rocket Disk except at the top and bottom, where it was attached to the outer wall with an axle.

The little man explained that when the rockets started, the outer shell of the disk revolved at a tremendous speed but the inside shell remained still. The Astral Rocket Disk went through the air like a—the little man consulted his luminous box for the right word. Finally he found it.

"Top!" he said. "No top," and he touched the top of his head, "no this TOP!"

The little man whirled himself around at a great speed and stopped suddenly.

"This top!" he said when he had recovered.

"But what do you use for power?" asked Eddie. "Where're your fuel tanks or dynamos or something? What makes the disk run?"

The little man frowned. "Disks no run. . . . Flies!"

"All right," said Eddie. "Flies! But I can't see how it flies. Where's the power?"

"Secret power," said the little man sternly.

"What secret power?" asked Eddie, as he looked around. Can't see any place to store your secret power around here."

The little man looked suspiciously at Eddie for a moment. He seemed to be thinking hard.

"You no dangerous," said the little man. "Here is secret power."

He walked over to the fat metal column in the center of the room and pressed an invisible button in its side. A small door sprang open in the column.

"Here, . . . look!" commanded the little man as he pointed to something in the column.

Eddie bent down and looked into the column. The little man's finger pointed to a flat spool of shiny metal wire. The spool of wire was about three inches across and one end of the wire was inserted into a small black box about the size of a box camera. The black box was attached to a metal rod that went up through the column.

"What!" exclaimed Eddie incredulously. "Is *that* your secret power?"

"Yes, this Zurianomatichrome Wire. We call this Secret Power Z," said the little man. "This wire explodes in vacuum. Box is vacuum. Secret Power Z makes powerful explosions. Carry through to rockets."

"Gosh! That must be like atomic energy, I betcha," said Eddie.

"Atomic energy!" the little man sneered. "Atomic energy very old-fashioned power. We Martineans stop use atomic power long ago. Now use Secret Power Z. Atomic power use only for"—the little man looked into his little box for the word—"yes, atomic power use for only . . . sewing machine!"

Eddie gulped and said, "Oh!"

Suddenly the little man looked at one of the clock-faced gadgets on the wall. Then he switched on the Interior-Exterior-Radar-Intercommunicator. The glass clouded and cleared, and Eddie found they were looking out at the orchard. The sun was directly overhead. The little man became very active and took out his tiny typewriter and banged away at the keys.

"Must make observations on your sun," he said by way of explanation.

"Say, it must be noon already," said Eddie. "I promised Grandma I'd tell her what happened up here. Look, I gotta go. I gotta . . . ."

And as Eddie made for the stairs the little man stopped him.

"What tell?" he demanded, angrily. "You see secret power. Now tell. You no go. Stop!"

He stood in front of Eddie menacingly.

"Lookit here, now," insisted Eddie. "I gotta go. I told my grandmother I'd be back and tell her about something. I'm not gonna tell her about your old secret power. Anyway, she wouldn't believe it if I told her." And Eddie started for the ladder again. But the little man put his hand against Eddie's chest. Eddie felt as though he were pushed up against a brick wall.

"I go with," said the little man. "Must protect secret power."

"All right then, c'mon," said Eddie impatiently. "Hurry up! My grandma's gonna be mad."

The little man eyed Eddie coldly. Then he quickly snapped open the column and tinkered inside it for a moment. He detached the spool of Zurianomatichrome Wire and the little black box. He clipped the black box to his belt and slipped the wire into one of his pockets.

"This also weapon," he said as he pointed to the little black box. "Is possible to destroy everything to horizon using Secret Power Z."

Eddie shivered. Then he said, nervously, "Well, don't point that thing at me. Are you ready now? Let's go."

"Ready. Go," said the little man and he let Eddie climb out of the Astral Rocket Disk. In a few minutes they sped down the hill to Eddie's grandmother's house.

"Eddie boy," she said as he burst into the kitchen. "Where have you been so long? I was getting worried. Has anything happened?"

"We-e-ll," Eddie began, "nothing happened to Grandfather's tree, if that's what you mean. But . . . ."

"And who is this little boy?" asked Eddie's grandmother as she saw the little man from Martinea standing in the doorway. "Come in, boy. Any friend of Eddie's is a friend of mine. What's your name?"

"He's a . . . he's a Martinean," said Eddie hesitatingly. "He just came along."

"What was that name?" asked his grandmother, as she put on her glasses. She seemed to hear better with her glasses on. "Martin . . . ?"

"Martin-e-an," repeated Eddie.

"Oh! Martin E. Ann," said Eddie's grandmother. "How nice. That's an unusual name. What's the 'E' stand for? We have some people around here who have first names for last names. There's Matilda T. George, . . . Joshua Elmer Irving . . . . So you're Martin E. Ann. H-mm, does the 'E' stand for Elmer? I'll just call you Marty. Come in, boys, come in. I've just baked some apple pies, and we're having corn fritters and apple pie for lunch. Now you show Marty where to wash up, Eddie, and I'll set another plate on the table."

4. SECRET POWER Z—LOST

Although corn fritters dripping with maple syrup and apple pie topped with whipped cream was Eddie's favorite lunch, he did not eat much. He was afraid the little man might say something or do something that would disturb his grandmother. So all through lunch Eddie talked and talked as he tried to keep his grandmother from asking any embarrassing questions, like what town the little man came from or what school he went to. Eddie talked about Grandfather's apple tree, about the Boy Scouts, about anything he could think of. Until his grandmother said, "Eddie, you've been chattering so much you haven't eaten your pie."

Eddie breathed a sigh of relief when lunch was over. And as his grandmother's back was turned when she carried away the lunch dishes, he jerked his head toward the door and whispered to the little man, "Let's get outside."

"Oh, Eddie," called his grandmother just as Eddie and the little man stepped out onto the porch.

"Yes, Grandma," said Eddie, and he whispered to the little man, "Wait here," and went into the house again.

"Eddie, be a good boy and run an errand for me, please," said his grandmother in a voice loud enough to be heard outside. "Eddie, I want you to go down to the general store. I'll write a note to Captain Jack. I don't want you to forget anything."

In a few minutes Eddie came out again to the little man waiting outside. The little man glowered as Eddie came out the door and put his hand against Eddie's chest.

"Stop! No go!" he said sternly.

"Huh?" said Eddie.

"No go! You no carry message about Secret

Power Z to General Store and Captain Jack, to United States military authority," said the little man in a tense voice as he pointed to Eddie's grandmother's note.

"Huh?" said Eddie again. His mouth hung open. Then he closed it with a snap as it dawned on him what the little man meant.

"Aw, cut that out. Nobody's gonna tell the United States Army or anybody else about your old Secret Power . . . . General store's not a general. It's a store where you buy things, general things—groceries and nails and post cards and things. And Captain Jack ain't a real captain. He keeps the store. Guess he was a corporal or something once. This is just a note for flour, sugar and raisins, and white thread."

The explanation seemed to satisfy the little man.

"Good!" he said. "I go with. You no tell about Secret Power."

They started down the road but they had not gone far before they again heard Eddie's grandmother's voice.

"Yoo-hoo, . . . Eddie! . . . Eddie!" she called from the front porch. "I've been thinking. . . . If your little friend's going to play around with you this afternoon he'd better change into a pair of your blue jeans. Marty, your ma isn't going to like it if you get that nice green suit all dusty. There's a pair of Eddie's jeans hanging on the barn door. You'd better change into them, Marty."

Eddie looked at the little man for a moment and worried what he was going to do.

"Good," said the little man and he nodded his head, to Eddie's amazement. "Where barn?"

Eddie led the way. They climbed over the fence which separated the barnyard from the road and they jumped over the little brook which ran alongside it, and they ran up to the barn. A few of the farm animals (the goat and a calf) and some of the geese stood around and watched as the little man changed into Eddie's blue jeans. He took off his green jacket and hung it on a nail in back of the door. Then he stuffed a lot of the instruments and gadgets, which he had carried in his jacket, into the pockets of the jeans. At last he snapped his black box onto his belt and indicated to Eddie he was ready.

"Good disguise—no?" He seemed pleased

with himself. "Look like native American boy. No?"

Eddie nodded, even though he thought the little man looked sort of strange with all his pockets so stuffed with gadgets they stuck out all over him and his jeans rolled up like shaggy tires around his ankles. Eddie had seen boys who looked like that before. "Ready? Come on," he said.

"One minute," said the little man. He bent over and began to adjust one of the knobs on his shoes. "Speed limit—forty miles!" he suggested.

"Now don't go doing that," insisted Eddie. "I'm not gonna run to the village. Nobody runs when they run on an errand. It's not natural."

The little man thought a moment as he looked up at Eddie. Then he nodded his agreement.

"Yes," he said. "Must walk slow like native American boy."

To Eddie's relief they met no one Eddie knew on the road down to the village, and there was no one but old Captain Jack himself in his general store and post office.

"Hot enough for you boys?" said Captain Jack as they came into the cool peppery-smelling shade of his store. Then after he read Eddie's grandmother's note he said, "Yes, sirree. I'll fill this order out before you can blink an eyelash. You can each help yourselves to one lemon drop out of that jar while I'm filling it. Remember, I just said just one lemon drop. And keep away from those boxes."

Eddie stood around uncomfortably sucking his lemon drop, praying silently that the little man would not do or say anything unusual. Fearfully, he watched as the little man wandered around the general store, looking at things and touching things.

"Eddie," said Captain Jack as he weighed out some sugar. "Did you hear about the Boy Scout Jamboree we're gonna have around here out at Miller's Pond? You're a Scout, aren't you?"

"I'm almost a second-class Scout," said Eddie. "Just gotta pass two more tests."

"Good boy. You'll make it, I bet," said Captain Jack. Then he turned to the little man. "What about you, young feller? You a Scout?"

Eddie answered quickly before the little man could say a word.

"Nope, not him. He's a stranger around here. Just got here yesterday."

"A foreigner, eh?" said Captain Jack. "W-e-ll, ought to be a Scout. Scoutin's good for you. Yessir, scoutin's good for boys."

"Right you are," said someone who came into the store just then. It was Mr. Pearson. Mr. Pearson was the principal of the village school, magistrate of the local court, a notary public and the scoutmaster of the village Boy Scout troop. He was a rather plump man, dressed as he always dressed during the summer months in his scouting uniform.

"Yes indeed, Captain Jack," he said. "You're absolutely right. Scouting makes fine men out of fine boys. Oh, hello, Eddie, and hello there. . . ." He nodded to the little man as he continued talking cheerfully.

"Eddie, has anyone told you about our Jamboree next Thursday out in the pasture alongside Miller's Pond?"

"Yessir," said Eddie. "Captain Jack has just been saying—"

"Well, I do hope you come out and get into

it," said Mr. Pearson. "Of course, you're not a member of our troop but I'll be glad to have you with us. I'd like to have you get into some of the races. Let's see how you city Scouts stand up against our country boys. Say, I just remembered you're a pretty good swimmer, Eddie. I guess you might walk off with maybe a second, or even a first prize ribbon!"

"Aw, I'm not that good," said Eddie blushing modestly.

"And your friend here," said Mr. Pearson, turning to the little man. "Troop 333 would like to have you come to our Jamboree, too. Come along next Thursday with Eddie. Now, Captain Jack, is there any mail for me?"

"Nothing!" said Captain Jack.

"Right you are. Well, good-bye. Remember, Thursday," said Mr. Pearson, and he snapped a three-fingered salute at Eddie and the little man and was gone.

"Gotta lotta pep, that man," said Captain Jack. "Here's your grandma's order, Eddie. I put it in two bags so you both can carry. Watch out you don't bust that bag of sugar."

Eddie took one bag and the little man, after a moment's hesitation, picked up the other.

"So long, Captain Jack," said Eddie.

"So long. Don't take any wooden nickels," said Captain Jack with a chuckle, as he waved them out the door.

The little man seemed thoughtful as he and Eddie plodded along the dusty road back to Eddie's grandmother's house. About halfway back he asked Eddie, "What is Boy Scouts?"

Eddie explained as best he could about the Boy Scouts—what the Scouts stood for, how to become a Scout, about good turns. And he told about the Scout Oath, the Scout Handshake, the Scout Salute, the three different Scout classes—tenderfoot, second-class and first-class Scout. And just as Eddie was beginning to explain about merit badges the little man interrupted him.

"Silence!" he commanded sharply as he looked up at the sky. There was the sound of an airplane off in the distance. Eddie could not see the plane and he could hardly hear it. The little man put down the package of groceries and hunted through his pockets. He had stuffed his equipment in the blue jeans so quickly he had forgotten where he had put things. Finally he found the little telescope and his little typewriting machine. For a moment he studied the distant plane through his telescope, then he ticked away at his typewriter. When he finished typing out his report on the airplane he had observed, he told Eddie to wait just one more minute.

"Must arrange equipment," he said. "This not efficient."

During the next few minutes the little man moved things around from one pocket in his jeans (or rather Eddie's jeans) to the other. But he stopped suddenly. He looked at Eddie with a most peculiar expression. His usually florid face had become a sickly white, then it turned to green. It was evident something was terribly wrong. His hands raced in and out of his pockets with amazing speed.

"Where is Zurianomatichrome Wire?" he gasped hopelessly. "Cannot find Zurianomatichrome Wire!"

"Gosh!" exclaimed Eddie. "You sure? Did you look carefully?"

The little man searched desperately through his pockets again.

"Zurianomatichrome Wire not here!" he said in a hollow voice.

"Maybe you dropped it . . . or something," said Eddie.

The little man said nothing for a moment. Then he swiftly bent down and twirled the knobs on his shoes.

"Must return to general store," he said quickly. "Speed limit sixty miles!"

And he grabbed Eddie's arm, and before Eddie could say a word he found himself flying along the road back to the village. Fortunately, there was no one along the road, no one in the village street and no one in Captain Jack's general store that hot afternoon. Perhaps everyone had gone fishing as the Captain had, because they found the door locked and a penciled note, tacked to the door, which said, "Gone fishing. They're biting in Kinderhook Creek."

But the locked door did not stop the little man. With one sharp tap of his finger he snapped the lock and rushed through the door. In a flash he was in the general store and he whirled about every which way, searching the floor, the counters, the barrels and the shelves. He did not let go of Eddie's arm when the door was opened and since he did not turn down the speed knobs of his shoes, they still traveled at the speed of sixty miles an hour.

In a few minutes the little man was satisfied that the spool of Zurianomatichrome Wire had not been dropped in Captain Jack's general store. Then he started up the road toward Eddie's grandmother's house again.

"Slow up!" shouted Eddie when he finally caught his breath. "You can't find anything speeding along like this."

"I can see quick!" said the little man grimly and he did not reduce his speed until they stood on Eddie's grandmother's front porch once more.

"Well! Well!" said Eddie's grandmother. "Now that was nice and prompt. You boys can have some cookies if you want some—cinnamon cookies."

"Grandma," said Eddie breathlessly, "did you find something?"

"What something?" asked Eddie's grandmother.

"Did you happen to see a spool of shiny wire around? My friend here lost it."

"A spool of wire. H-m-m, . . . a spool of shiny wire?" asked Eddie's grandmother.

"Why, yes. I think I remember seeing one lying around somewhere. Now where did I see that spool of wire?"

Eddie's grandmother tapped her forehead, rubbed her chin, looked up over her glasses, down under them, and then she rolled her eyes toward the ceiling. The little man and Eddie waited with bated breath.

"Let me see now. Was it on the porch? . . . No-o. . . . On the lawn? No-o. . . . Oh, I remember. On the barn floor! Your friend Marty must have dropped it as he was getting into your jeans. Yes, that's where I saw it. I saw it on the barn floor. I'd gone out there to get some baling wire and . . . ."

But the little man did not wait to find out what Eddie's grandmother wanted to get in the barn. He ran for the barn with the speed of the wind.

"My! My!" gasped Eddie's grandmother. "Somebody *is* in a hurry."

"That wire's terribly important to him, Grandma," explained Eddie just before he too raced off to the barn.

Eddie's grandmother looked after them and chuckled.

"Dear, dear. Boys do decide some of the strangest things are terribly important sometimes. Dear, dear, all this fuss over a little spool of wire."

5. THE SEARCH

Like a whirlwind the little man had already gone through the barn before Eddie got there. The barnyard was in an uproar. The hens cackled, the geese hissed, the ducks quacked, the calf mooed and the goat raced around looking for someone to butt. The big gander stood with wings spread, neck outstretched, hissing angrily in the barn door. He stabbed at Eddie with his beak, as Eddie came through the door, and missed him by a fraction.

Eddie found the little man scurrying back and forth across the floor of the barn on his hands and knees. He was inspecting every inch of the barn floor through his high-powered telescope. He looked (Eddie thought) very much like a large nervous mouse, darting across the floor that way.

Suddenly he stopped and concentrated his telescope on one spot on the floor. He adjusted the telescope quickly and again peered through it at the same spot.

"Find something?" asked Eddie.

The little man turned his head, then he straightened up and pointed stiffly to the spot he had been looking at.

"Microscopic dust of Zurianomatichrome," he said dramatically. "Secret Power Z wire rest on floor here!" Then he went back to inspecting the floor which surrounded that spot. He worked carefully, swiftly, in an ever-widening circle. Again he stopped. He was very excited.

"What you got?" asked Eddie as he crouched down beside the little man.

"Large fragments of Secret Power Z wire here!" he shouted in a horror-stricken voice. "Someone cut wire here!"

"Someone cut wire here *today!*" he repeated. His voice had risen to a shriek.

"Dear me, yes. I cut it!" said Eddie's grandmother as she stood in the doorway. "That's just when I came over to tell you. I just remembered I did see that spool of wire here as I came looking for the baling wire. I had to fix the hole in the screen door you'd pushed into it, Eddie. Well, I couldn't find any baling wire and I did see that little spool of shiny wire and I snipped a short length of it with my sewing scissors. I do hope you don't mind, Marty. It was just a little piece."

It seemed to Eddie that the little man did mind! He minded very much. He jumped to his feet, his eyes flashing angrily and his mouth pressed down in a thin line. He was bursting with rage!

"Grandma," said Eddie in desperation before the little man exploded. "What did you do with the spool after you snipped the wire? And, Grandma, was there anyone else in the barn?"

"Why, I just put it right back where I found it," said his grandmother. "Did you say was there anyone else around the barn, Eddie? Why, no! Let me see . . . . No, no one except this old gander. Shoo away, you (she snapped her apron at the old gander as she spoke). Yes, this silly old gander was strutting around the barn and some of the baby ducks. But I didn't see anyone else. Now, Marty, don't you feel too bad about it. I think if you look carefully I'm sure you'll find it."

With that consoling thought Eddie's grandmother left them in the barn as she went hunting a nest of eggs the old leghorn hen had hidden away out in the bushes.

Eddie stole a side glance at the little man. He was still boiling mad, but his anger had cooled a little. For just one moment, as his grandmother talked, it seemed to Eddie that the little man's hand had moved toward the black box that hung on his belt. What if he had pointed that box, which he said "could destroy anything to the horizon," at Eddie's grandmother! What could Eddie do? What could anyone do? Eddie's mouth became dry with horror at the thought of it!

"Where screen door?" demanded the little man sharply.

"Guess Grandma meant the screen door to the kitchen," said Eddie. "I came through it fast yesterday and I guess I must have ripped it a little. I was gonna fix it but . . . ."

The little man had stopped listening to Eddie. He was looking suspiciously at the old gander who had returned to stare in at them again from the doorway.

"This bird live here long?" he asked Eddie in a very low voice.

"Yeah, guess he has," Eddie answered. "Ever since I remember. Why?"

The little man kept studying the old gander a few more seconds. Then he took out his little dictionary box and he ruffled through the luminous cards. He seemed to be looking for a number of words. At last he snapped it shut. He began speaking very carefully, weighing each word.

"Do . . . United States Army . . . train . . . goosebirds . . . like train pigeon-birds and dogs . . . to spy in war?" he hissed sharply.

"Say! What are you talking about?" Eddie almost shouted. "Listen here, that old goose is my grandmother's goose gander. He's been here for years, long as I can remember. And the United States Army ain't training any gooses—geeses—geese, I mean, to spy in war! Or carrier pigeons or dogs either. Lookit here! Nobody around here is spying."

The little man listened with his mouth clamped shut.

"Lookit here," continued Eddie. "I'm real

sorry you lost your spool of Zurianomati . . . er . . . what-ever-you-call-it wire. And I'm willing to help you hunt around and find it. But don't go getting mad at people and geese. Nobody wants to hurt you and don't you go around looking to hurt anybody else. That box there now if you go pointing that at people."

The little man looked down at the box. Suddenly the look of anger left his face and he looked sad, sadder than Eddie had ever seen him.

"This no longer weapon," he said slowly. "With no Zurianomatichrome, this no power." And the little man pointed to his non-gravity shoes, the bracelet on his wrist and all the other machines he carried in his pockets. "With no Secret Power Z, this no power." He sadly shook his head.

"But how come they have been working right along?" asked Eddie.

"Will work for small time," said the little man. "Must recharge with Zurianomatichrome Power regular, or no work."

"Oh! Like an electric battery, I guess. You gotta recharge it," said Eddie. "This Secret Power Z might be like an extra-supercharged electricity."

The little man was too downcast to confirm or deny Eddie's latest guess on the secret power of Zurianomatichrome. Suddenly as he thought of something he started for the door.

"Where you going?" asked Eddie. "The spool of wire must be here someplace."

"Screen door!" shouted the little man before he dashed out of the barn. In a few minutes he was back. He held a length of the shiny wire. It was about a foot and a half long. Still clinging to the Secret Power Z wire were a few corroded black shreds of the screen door. He must have ripped it out of the kitchen door fast.

"Here is piece of Secret Power Z wire," he said triumphantly. He seemed pleased there was so much of it.

"Bet he wished Grandma had snipped more," said Eddie to himself. And as Eddie watched the little man insert one end of the wire first into a tiny hole in the side of each of his shoes, he explained to Eddie, "Now charged with Zurianomatichrome Power. Each machine with very small vacuum box."

Then he charged his bracelet, his tiny pin-wheel helicopter and the various other little machines in his pocket. He started to insert the wire in the little black box hanging on his belt, then he looked at Eddie and changed his mind. He did not charge his terrible weapon with Zurianomatichrome Power.

Eddie breathed a sigh of relief and grinned. It looked as if the little man was beginning to get the idea that Eddie and his grandmother and everyone else in the United States were friendly people (and friendly geese) and that he did not need his terrible weapon.

"No charge black vacuum box," said the little man. "Use too much Zurianomatichrome Power."

He held up the wire for Eddie to see. More than one-third of the shiny wire had been used up charging all the little vacuum boxes in his equipment.

"Now look for Zurianomatichrome Wire," said the little man, and he and Eddie searched every nook and cranny of the barn and barnyard.

The afternoon wore on. They hunted high and they hunted low. After they'd searched through the hay in the hayloft for the third time Eddie wanted to quit.

"Lookit here," he said finally. "It's hot up here and I've got some chores to do and I've gotta get my supper. Gotta get Grandma's cow out of the pasture. What do you say we look for the wire tomorrow?"

The little man went on searching through the hayloft without saying a word for a moment or two.

"What harm can it do if we don't find the wire today?" Eddie insisted. "Gosh, the wire's here somewheres. It can't do any harm if we wait till tomorrow."

The little man looked up at Eddie.

"What is harm?" he asked. Then he consulted his little box with the luminous cards.

"Harm means like dangerous, no?" he said.

"Well, sort of," said Eddie. Then a thought almost set him in a panic. "Say, wait a minute. Is this wire dangerous laying around like that? Like that radium stuff, I mean, you know radioactivity and things like that?"

The little man shook his head emphatically.

"No! Much superior material," he said proudly. "No harm, no danger. Zurianomatichrome no explode except in vacuum boxes made by Martinean scientist. Only harm is for Zurianomatichrome. Must find wire now!"

And he went back to his search as if his explanation had closed the subject.

"What kinda harm could happen to the wire if we don't find it right now?" asked Eddie impatiently.

"Secret Power Z can no stand Earth Moisture," said the little man seriously. Then since Eddie looked doubtful he got out his little dictionary box again and looked through it quickly until he found a card which he read.

"Earth Moisture, United States America—Ice, Water, Soda Pop, Lemonade, Root Beer, Dew . . . ."

"Oh!" said Eddie. "You mean if you don't get it under a dry cover before nightfall and the dew begins to settle . . . ?"

The little man nodded before Eddie had finished his question.

"Yes, Zurianomatichrome Wire lose power if touches Earth Moisture," he said and went back to work.

"Well, . . . Gosh . . . . Well, I'm sorry," said Eddie slowly, "but I gotta go. Gotta do my chores. So long. Hope you find it."

The little man did not answer. He kept right on searching frantically. And he was still in the barn, walking along one of the beams (hanging head down the way Eddie had first seen him), when Eddie brought his grandmother's cow, Bessie, in from pasture about sunset.

"Any luck? Did you find your wire?" asked Eddie gently.

The little man looked down at Eddie and shook his head. Then he marched along the rafter, down the wall and quietly sat down on the barn floor.

"Grandma says you can have supper with us if you'll come up to the house." Again the little man sadly shook his head.

"And she says you can bunk up in my room if you want to. I told her about your sleeping there last night."

The little man shook his head once more.

"Must return to Astral Rocket Disk," he said wearily. "Must contact Martinea. Must report emergency."

He took the short piece of Secret Power Z wire from his pocket.

"No much power left," he said sadly. "Maybe no contact Martinea."

And that was the last thing he said before he went out of the barn, traveling at only five miles an hour to save the power in his non-gravity shoes. And it was at that speed that he slowly went up the road toward the orchard.

That night when Eddie's grandmother said, as they sat on the porch, "Look, Eddie, look at the sky. There's some summer lightning up over the ridge back of Grandfather's apple tree. It's just a flicker of lightning. It must be some far-off storm," Eddie did not say anything.

He knew better. He knew that the weak flicker of bluish light was not lightning. It was the signals the little man was trying to send out to Martinea. And he felt sorry for the little man alone in his space ship, because anyone could see those signals would never reach across the great distance to Martinea. They were hardly strong enough to be seen on Eddie's grandmother's front porch.

6. THE BLUE LIGHT

Before sunup next morning, even before the roosters got up to call the sun, everybody who lived on Eddie's grandmother's farm was awake! The little man was back searching the barn again. And all the fowls and animals who lived in the barn were squawking, clucking, mooing. All raised their voices in protest at being shaken out of their beds and pushed off their roosts in the dark hours of the morning.

Right after breakfast Eddie ran over to the barn to help search for the lost Zurianomatichrome Wire. The little man did not speak or look at Eddie as he came in the door. He had already searched and re-searched the barn for hours. Now he appeared discouraged and he moved slowly around the barn floor pushing a wisp of straw with his foot now and then. Eddie moved with much more spirit than the little man did. He began once again to move the bags of feed. They had gone through the feed bags twice yesterday. It was harder doing it alone. Eddie turned to call the little man to give him a hand. After all it was his spool of wire they were looking for.

And as he turned from the feed bin some strange something caught his eye.

"Hey! What's that?" he cried. He pointed with excitement to a curious blue light which glowed from certain spots on the barn floor.

The little man turned and looked at the spots Eddie pointed to, and he just shrugged his shoulders.

"This natural," he said in a lifeless voice. "This where fragments of Zurianomatichrome Wire touch floor. This light comes after Zurianomatichrome Power is thin. Soon will disappear. Maybe one, maybe two day. Use thin power to light interior Astral Rocket Disk."

Eddie remembered the cool blue light

which came from the walls of the inner room in the space ship and said, "Oh!"

Now that the little man had talked, Eddie tried to keep the conversation going in an effort to cheer him up. Eddie asked him as gently as he could if he had contacted Martinea. The little man just shook his head and said nothing. Eddie said other things, but since he could get no response, he gave it up. He tried whistling quietly as he searched for the wire. And after a while he just quit whistling, too.

The big old gander came hissing pompously into the barn and broke the silence. The little man threw a dark scornful glance over his shoulder at the gander and turned back to his work. But suddenly, he turned quickly to the gander again with a piercing glare.

"STOP!" he shouted as he ran for the bewildered bird.

The old gander stood his ground firmly and hissed his defiance. But the rush of the little man was too much for him and he turned to flee. He was too late. The little man had an unbreakable grip around the old gander's neck.

"Hey there!" shouted Eddie, scrambling out of the feed box. "What are you doing there?

Let go of my grandmother's gander. . . . What goes on?"

"Look!" screamed the little man as he forced the frightened gander's head around with one hand and he pointed with the other. "Look! . . . Look! . . . Sign of Zurianomatichrome on bird mouth!"

Eddie looked and sure enough, it was there! Along the beak of the old gander was the blue-tinged light! The sign of thin Zurianomatichrome power!

"What do you know? . . . Gosh, . . ." he said softly. "Gosh, do you think he ate up the wire?"

"Will see," said the little man grimly as he hunted in his pockets for one of his instruments. "Hold bird!"

Eddie got a tight grip on the old gander's neck.

"Now, listen, you're not going to cut open— You're not going to hurt this old gander, are you?" he asked anxiously.

"No hurt," promised the little man, adjusting a knob on his telescope. "This X-Ray Microscope Telescope."

"O.K. I'll hold him," said Eddie. "I got a good grip on him now."

But the big gander thought differently and he swung his huge wings and wrenched himself free of Eddie's arms. His free right wing threw Eddie into one corner of the barn and his left one sent the little man sprawling. Then hissing and honking hysterically he raced in dizzy wild circles around the barn with Eddie and the little man in hot pursuit.

They made many wild grabs at the big gander but with no success. Finally, they cornered him in Bessie's stall.

"Attack together!" cried the little man.

And they both threw themselves at the same moment at the cornered gander.

"Got him!" gasped Eddie breathlessly.

"Now will see Zurianomatichrome Wire inside goose bird yes or no," said the little man.

He pressed the larger end of his X-Ray Microscope Telescope against the top of the bird's head and peered into the smaller end of it. Then still peering through his telescope he moved it down the neck of the bird, down along his back to the tip of his tail.

"Find it?" asked Eddie eagerly.

The little man stood up and shook his head.

"No Zurianomatichrome Wire in goose bird," he said. His voice was tragic.

"Gosh! Well, how come—" Eddie started to say but something happened that made him shout out, "Hey, grab the goat! Lookit the goat! His whiskers! He's got the blue light!"

The little man whirled in the nick of time to grab the horns of the goat, who (through curiosity) had stuck his head around the wall to watch them examine the old gander.

"Stop! No go!" cried the little man as he tugged at the struggling goat. "Here signs of Zurianomatichrome Wire, too. Hold goat!"

Eddie let go of the gander and got a good grip on the goat. The goat butted forward and tugged backward but Eddie hung on as the little man gave the goat the X-Ray Microscope Telescope treatment.

But even though the blue light glowed from the goat's whiskers, the tip of his nose, his lips and his front teeth after the examination the little man heaved a sigh and said there were no traces of the lost wire inside the goat.

"Are you sure? You mean there's none at all in the goat?" exclaimed Eddie.

The little man shook his head.

"Well, how come?" said Eddie. "Gosh, that old goat chews anything and everything—paper, tin cans. I've even seen him nibbling on the screen door once. He might have chewed up the wire."

"No! no Zurianomatichrome in goat," repeated the little man. "Let goat go."

Eddie let the goat go and as they watched him scamper out to the barnyard Eddie had a thought.

"Say, I betcha I know what happened. Betcha both of them nibbled a little on the wire. Maybe one of them carried it away somewhere. I have seen the old gander walking around the barnyard dangling a piece of wood or something in his beak sometimes. And I've seen this old goat doing the same thing, just carrying something around sort of absent-minded like. Betcha that's what happened. One of them carried it somewhere and then they just dropped it."

The little man looked at Eddie with a surprised expression on his face. Then he dug into his little dictionary box to find a special word among its luminous cards.

"Detective! You good detective!" he said graciously. "Yes, this possible. Goose bird or goat walk with wire some place. Now I must be good detective. Must follow goose bird and goat to find wire."

And that's what he did. For the next few days the little man shadowed the goose and the goat. He tiptoed or ran after them wherever they went. It was very difficult because the goose and the goat rarely went anywhere together or at the same time. The little man would race after one, then race after the other.

Sometimes shadowing one he'd keep track of the other by watching him through his telescope. Eddie helped him, too, sometimes and he did what he could to explain away the strange behavior of the little man to his grandmother. He told her that the little man (whom she always called Marty) was very interested in the goose and the goat. He had never seen a goose or a goat before and that there were no geese or goats in the place where the little man came from. Of course all that was true.

And Eddie's grandmother said, "Oh, the poor boy! Never to have ever seen geese or goats before. Oh, the poor boy!"

7. THE SPACE SHIP EARTHBOUND

The blueberries that grew in the big patch back of the orchard had ripened all at once and Eddie had to go berry-picking. His grandmother canned the berries and made blueberry pies and muffins. It was Eddie's job to pick them when they ripened every summer. So he did not see much of the little man while he shadowed the goat and the goose. He would have liked to help the little man because he felt sorry for him but he did not have the time.

The little man spent the daylight hours usually chasing the goat. The goat ranged free all over the farm. But the goose stuck close to the barnyard. He had a regular line of march through and around the barnyard down to the brook and back again. The little man could watch the goose from a distance with his telescope as he chased the goat. In the late afternoon the goat stayed in the barnyard so he was able to watch them both in the same place at the same time.

After his berry-picking Eddie joined the little man as he sat quietly down by the brook watching the big gander waddle around in the shallow waters. He would sit beside him and try to get the little man to talk. But with little success. The little man was usually too weary (from chasing the goat) to talk much. Eddie talked about scouting and about his friends in New York and things like that. Sometimes they would sit together and say nothing for a long while.

It seemed to Eddie that the little man should not be called Marty. He couldn't get himself to call him Marty as his grandmother did. Somehow the little man reminded Eddie of a story he had once read about a man named Icarus who tried to fly with a pair of homemade wings. The wings came apart and

Icarus fell to earth. Eddie could not remember how the story ended.

But he thought that Icarus must have felt like the little man felt now that he was grounded and had lost the power to fly in his space ship. And he decided if he were to give the little man a name he would have called him Icarus . . . or maybe Icky for short.

One evening as they sat at the edge of the brook, Eddie dangled a piece of branch in the water. He would stir up the muddy bottom and pick up dead leaves or some such rubbish with the tip of his stick and he would let it splash back into the water.

"You know," he said, "maybe you ought to do something else for a while. Want to come picking berries with me?"

The little man shook his head.

"How about fishing? We can catch some bullheads up the brook a way."

The little man shook his head again.

"Grandma asked me about you the other day. Says she's seen you around the barnyard . . . wants you to stop in for supper sometime."

Still the little man did not say anything. He had been living up in the orchard in his space ship and when Eddie had asked him what he ate (since he did look rather peaked) he said he ate concentrated food.

"Look, there's no sense moping around," said Eddie, digging away with his stick in the brook bottom. "If you can't find that Secret Power Z wire, you can't find it. So . . . ."

Eddie's stick had dug up a large mass of muck from the brook and as he was just about to let it splash back into the water the little man came to life and grabbed the stick from his hand.

"Stop!" he cried, all excited. "Look! Look on end stick!"

He pointed to the mass of muck. There, looped around the tip of the stick covered with old leaves and twigs, was the long-lost spool of Zurianomatichrome Wire!

It was not shiny any more. Eddie would hardly have recognized it, the spool of wire was now so dull and black.

"What'd you know!" shouted Eddie. "It's been here all along. Bet the old gander brought it down here."

The little man jumped to his feet and quickly cleaned away the debris that clung to the spool of wire. Then after carefully drying it as well as he could on Eddie's jeans (which he still wore) he took a little gaugelike instrument from one of his pockets. He placed the tip of the wire in the gauge and watched the needle on the face of the instrument. The needle did not budge at all. It did not even quiver!

"No power," said the little man bitterly. "All power gone. Earth Moisture kill power in Zurianomatichrome."

"Gosh," said Eddie gently, as he put his hand on the little man's shoulder. "I'm terribly sorry. Gosh, that's too bad."

The little man without a word shook Eddie's hand off his shoulder, turned his back and slowly walked away toward the apple orchard. Eddie tried to think of something to say to cheer him up but he could not. He looked after him for a while, then he went up to his grandmother's house and sat on the porch.

"Grandma," he said, when his grandmother came out and sat on her rocker, "my friend found his spool of wire."

"Oh, I'm so glad, Eddie," she said. "So glad for him, I mean. He's been so anxious to find it and so down-hearted, it seems to me.

Couldn't get him to say a word whenever I saw him."

"Guess he's not much happier now," said Eddie.

"Why?" asked his grandmother. "He wanted that spool of wire pretty bad, but for the life of me I can't tell why. Well, now he's got it."

"Not much good now, he says. Found it in the brook and he says it's all spoiled. . . ."

"Dear me, that is too bad," said Eddie's grandmother and she clucked her tongue. "Eddie, I'll tell you what. That little boy is lonesome. Now I know enough about boys to tell when a boy is lonesome. I think you ought to introduce him to some of your friends. Do you know where he lives?"

"Well, . . . he lives up that way," said Eddie slowly, pointing in the general direction of Grandfather's apple tree and the planet Martinea.

"Now I'll tell you what you do," said his grandmother. "Tomorrow morning never mind about the berries. I've enough to start my canning. You go up to see that boy and let me see . . . . Here now, why don't you take him to the Boy Scout Jamboree? . . . Remember you said Mr. Pearson invited you, even though you are a New York City Boy Scout. I'm sure he'd not mind to have another boy. . . . I'll put up a lunch for you both. . . ."

Eddie sat and thought a while.

"Maybe that is a good idea," said Eddie. "I'm not too sure he'll come along, but I'll ask him."

"That's it. You ask him," said Eddie's grandmother. "I'm sure Marty will enjoy the fun—the marshmallow roasts and all."

And after saying good-night to his grandmother, Eddie went to bed wondering how you ask a Martinean Scientist Explorer to come along to roast marshmallows at a village Boy Scout Jamboree.

Early next morning Eddie found the little man sitting glumly at the entrance to his space ship.

"Hi!" said Eddie, as he stood at the edge of the gully in back of Grandfather's apple tree.

The little man nodded and said nothing.

"Can I come aboard the disk?" asked Eddie.

The little man nodded again and pointed to

a strong branch which rested on the edge of the gully with its other end resting on the entrance to the space ship.

"Walk!" he said. "No waste Secret Power Z for helicopter."

Eddie balanced himself carefully and walked along the branch till he got to the disk entrance. He sat down on the rim and looked down into the space ship.

"Say, it's dark in there," he said.

The little man nodded.

"No Zurianomatichrome Power. No light from wall," he said.

"You mean to tell me you've been coming up here and going to sleep in the dark every night?" exclaimed Eddie in a shocked voice. Then after a moment of silence he suggested hesitantly, "I can lend you an old stable lantern . . . if you don't mind something that uses kerosene in your space ship."

The little man looked off into the distance and said nothing.

"Lookit here," said Eddie. "You've gotta cheer up or something. Lookit, my grandmother says . . . . Well, say, do you remember that man, Mr. Pearson, the scoutmaster we met in the general store? Remember, he says we could come to the Boy Scout Jamboree? . . . D'you wanta go?"

The little man still said nothing.

"Listen," said Eddie, impatient with the little man's silence. "If you're gonna mope around here like this, all right, but it seems to me you said you came here to explore America. Well, you can't do any exploring just sitting around like this. And you won't know anything about America if you don't know more Americans. You know just me and Grandma and her goat and the goose and the cow . . . and . . . well, all the Boy Scouts are Americans and you could . . . ."

Eddie talked on for some time. And it seemed after a half hour or so either his arguments convinced the little man, or he was just tired of listening to Eddie's voice, for he stood up suddenly and said, "Yes, . . . I go!"

8. THE BOY SCOUT JAMBOREE

The Boy Scout Jamboree was in full swing by the time Eddie and the little man arrived. Eddie wore his Scout uniform and his grandmother had found Eddie's old Cub Scout shirt for the little man to wear, so he would not feel out of place at the Jamboree.

There were three tents pitched in the pasture alongside Miller's Pond. Each tent had a cardboard sign pinned on its front flap, which gave the number of the Scout troop using the tent for its headquarters. And each tent had a troop flag flying from a pole. Eddie found Mr. Pearson, the scoutmaster, blowing a whistle in front of Troop 333's tent. He took the whistle out of his mouth long enough to greet Eddie and the little man with a cheery "Hello, Scouts" and a snappy three-fingered salute.

"All right, Scouts," shouted Mr. Pearson. "Troop 333 . . . All the Scouts of Troop 333 gather round here, please. . . . No fooling around now, fellows, we are ready to begin the races."

The Scouts of 333 came from all directions to gather in a circle around Mr. Pearson. The four patrol leaders helped quiet the twenty-five members of Troop 333 with their whistles. It took a few minutes before the hubbub quieted down and Mr. Pearson could be heard.

"Now, Scouts," he said, "this year I'd like to see Troop 333 walk off with the honors. Last year, you will remember, we did not do as . . . well, let's not dig up . . . Let bygones be bygones. Let's forget last year, Scouts. Let's remember this year. I want you to go out there and win. Now let me see. Who signed up for the three-legged race?"

A few of the Scouts raised their hands.

"Here, here," said Mr. Pearson. "We can make a better showing than that. What about you, Blubber, and you, Curly? You'll make a good three-legged team. . . . And Eddie, since you're a guest of Troop 333, sign up for the three-legged with your friend here. You ought to team up fine."

Eddie looked at the little man and started to say something but Mr. Pearson went on talking. "The hundred-yard dash—who's in the hundred-yard . . . ?" he went on. And in a very few minutes Mr. Pearson had arranged teams and cajoled a number of the laggards in Troop 333 to sign up for a lot of running, jumping, swimming and other contests which many of the modest village boys were sure they could never win.

Eddie found he was committed to three foot races, four swimming races, a cooking contest, a putting-up-and-taking-down-a-tent contest, a first-aid contest, and was one on the team (along with the rest of the troop) in the big tug-of-war that would end the athletic program that afternoon.

The little man had a lighter burden to bear. Perhaps because he wore Eddie's Cub Scout shirt Mr. Pearson thought he was younger and less experienced than the others. But the little man was assigned to the three-legged race (teamed with Eddie), the hundred-yard dash, the potato-sack race, the tracking-and-stalking contest, the tug-of-war and one swimming race, "the underwater free style" (whatever that was). Eddie promised the little man he would find out and explain it to him before the race began.

The little man had accepted his assignments with no protest, to Eddie's amazement. And when the Scouts lined up to have their names written down by one of the patrol leaders, who made a list of the contestants, Eddie had another shock. The little man stood in line in front of Eddie.

"Next Scout, . . . you," said the patrol leader, pointing to the little man. "Oh, you're a Cub, huh? All right, let's see that sleeve. I'll copy it off. Let's see, Den No. 1, Pack 5530. O.K., Cub . . . Just a second, what's your name?"

Eddie started to interfere.

"He hasn't been here long. He can't speak English much," said Eddie hastily.

But the little man brushed him aside and spoke for himself.

"Name, Marty!" he said in a clear, calm voice.

Eddie swallowed a lump. "Gosh, what d'you know," he said to himself. "Grandma's name stuck. What d'you know!"

After the starting-a-fire-with-two-matches contest (for tenderfoots) and after a number of other contests which had to do with scouting were run off, the athletic contests began.

This Boy Scout Jamboree was a lot different than the jamborees Eddie had attended with his own New York Scout troop. There were contests he had never seen in other jamborees. For example, there was a cow-milking contest and some of the big Scouts in the other two troops had a log-rolling contest out in the pond. It was a lot of fun and the little man seemed to enjoy everything, too, though he never laughed out loud and smiled only occasionally.

Eddie explained everything as slowly and as simply as he could so that the little man would not have to get out his dictionary box. When they finally got down to the regular athletic contests, everything was easy as far as Eddie was concerned. He did not have to explain running and jumping. Everything went along smoothly until the potato-sack race. The little man was entered in that race. Eddie helped him into his potato sack and told him what to do, to hop, holding his sack, until he crossed the finish line.

The race was started, and all the Scouts in that contest began hopping and flopping and tumbling over, like everyone always does when they compete in a potato-sack race. There was a lot of laughter and cheers from the sidelines. It seemed everyone, both the Scouts in the race and everyone watching it, was having a good time, everyone, that is, except the little man. As he hopped and tumbled and rolled behind all the other racers, Eddie saw that the little man was getting angrier and angrier. Finally Eddie saw him reach into one of his pockets, pull out his little Radiomatic Helicopter Minature, set the wheel of it spinning, and he was lifted and swept to the finish line in an instant!

There was so much confusion, laughter and excitement no one but Eddie noticed how the little man won that race. He was cheered and seemed proud of himself when Eddie ran up to help him crawl out of the potato sack.

"You shouldn't have done it," whispered Eddie as he knelt down by the side of the little man. "Marty, that wasn't fair."

The little man lifted his eyebrows. "What means fair?" he asked calmly.

And before he could fumble out his dictionary box, Eddie stopped him.

"Don't pull that out," Eddie whispered. "Fair means . . . well, if you win because you got something to help you win no one else has . . . well, that isn't fair."

The little man frowned and did not say anything for a moment.

"Win is important—yes?" he asked in a low voice.

"Win is important—yes, if you win fair!" said Eddie. "If you don't win fair—no!"

As they stood on the sidelines, watching some other races, Eddie explained more about playing and winning fair like a Boy Scout. At last the little man nodded his head.

"Yes, now I win fair," he promised.

"All out for the three-legged race!" somebody shouted.

"We're in that, Marty," said Eddie. "Come along . . . ."

At the starting line Eddie tied his right leg to the little man's left leg and with their arms thrown over each other's shoulders they were ready to begin the three-legged race.

"Remember now," said Eddie out of the side of his mouth. "Win fair."

The little man nodded.

Mr. Pearson blew his whistle and there was a chorus of blasts from the whistles of the other scoutmasters and all the patrol leaders.

"Quiet, everybody!" shouted Mr. Pearson, when everyone was already quiet. "Now, Scouts, in this race you three-legged teams must run from this starting line to that white birch tree, around the tree, and back here again. Is that understood?"

All the three-legged teams nodded their heads.

"All right! . . . One to get set, . . . two to get ready, . . . and three to go!" shouted Mr. Pearson, and with a wave of the signal flag he held, the race was on.

Eddie and the little man started off at the same clumsy pace as the other teams. But suddenly Eddie felt his right leg (the one that was tied to the little man's left one) jerked forward, and lickety-split they had raced across the field, round the birch tree and were back to the starting line—the winners of the three-legged race!

The other teams had hardly started. None of them had hopped more than three feet from the starting line.

Deafening cheers and shouts greeted their astounding victory.

"What a team!" chortled Mr. Pearson. "I knew you would make a wonderful team!"

The little man had bent down quickly when they reached the finishing line (or starting line), the moment they crossed it, or they would have run past Mr. Pearson. Eddie bent with him and untied the string that held their legs together. He saw the little man turn back the knob on his non-gravity shoes to zero! It had been turned to the eighty-mile speed limit mark!

"That was not fair," whispered Eddie, his face flushed with embarrassment at the undeserved cheers they were getting.

The little man scowled.

"I no turn knob to eighty-mile speed limit,"

he said calmly. "Accident. You push knob with foot."

Eddie for a moment was undecided. Should he or should he not try to explain why the little man and he could not accept the honor of having won the three-legged race? But the next race had already started (the wheelbarrow race) and no one was paying any attention to them any more.

When the swimming races came along, Eddie did pretty well. He won a first ribbon, a couple of seconds, and an honorable mention (for effort, said Mr. Pearson) in the backstroke race.

The little man won the "underwater free style"! Eddie hoped it was a clean win but he wasn't too sure. The little man, although he did wear a borrowed pair of trunks (Eddie's trunks, which flapped loosely around his wiry little body), looked very strange as he waited with the others for the starting signal, because he insisted on wearing his thick-soled nongravity shoes in the race.

There was no law anyone could think of why he should not wear his shoes into the water if he wanted to. And after a little discussion between the scoutmasters, the underwater-free-style race began.

The object of the race was to swim from one side of the narrow neck of the pond to the other. The contestants were to swim the twelve-foot stretch underwater all the way. They could use whatever swimming style they preferred—dog paddle, breast stroke, Australian crawl.

"You can even walk," laughed Mr. Pearson just before he started the race, "as long as we do not see your pointed little heads sticking out of the water until you get over to the other bank!"

Everybody laughed uproariously with Mr. Pearson.

One to get set . . . two to get ready . . . three to go . . . and they were off!

The little man dived in just an instant after the others. But in a flash his head bobbed up from the water at the other side of the pond and he clambered up on the bank!

"Ray-y-y, Marty!" screamed everyone. "What a man, Marty!"

Everybody cheered except Eddie. He did not say a word.

At the end of the Jamboree, after the Scouts

had sung some scouting songs, the ribbons were awarded to the winners. Mr. Pearson made a short speech about scouting and fair play and then those Scouts who had won honors were called up. When Marty was called up he stepped forward, took his ribbons, looked at them a moment, then he thrust them back into Mr. Pearson's hand!

He pointed to himself and said, "No good Scout!"

And he turned and walked away. Eddie chased after him. Mr. Pearson was surprised but since he had a lot of other ribbons to give out he went right on.

The little man and Eddie walked up the road toward Eddie's grandmother's farm in silence. The little man spoke just once during their walk.

"Earth Moisture, Water, no good for non-gravity shoes," he said solemnly.

"Oh," said Eddie. Now he understood why the little man had to use special power to get out of the pond in the underwater-free-style race.

Just before they parted at the apple orchard Eddie showed the little man the Boy Scout grip and then he put out his hand.

"You know what, Marty?" said Eddie. "I think you're a good Scout—shake!"

And Eddie and the little man shook hands . . . like Boy Scouts shake hands.

9. THE STRANGE STORM

The strangest storm that Captain Jack ever remembered struck in mid-afternoon on the last day of August.

"I've lived in this county, man and boy, for nigh onto eighty years, Eddie," said Captain Jack, "and I'm here to tell you that's the strangest storm that ever hit this county. It sure was a whopper!"

If Eddie had loitered one minute on his way down to Captain Jack's to get some weather stripping and the weekly newspaper for his grandmother, he would have been caught in that storm out on the open road. No sooner had he entered the general store, when it struck. Captain Jack came rushing out from behind his counter as Eddie came in the door, shouting, "Shut that door! There's a whopper a-coming! Look at that black cloud out there! . . . WHAM!"

Eddie whirled in his tracks and he, too, saw the weird black cloud that was the talk of the village for months to come. No one could agree on the shape of it. Some said it was the shape of an umbrella. Others thought it looked like an immense mushroom, and there were those who thought (as Eddie did) it looked exactly like a fat, gigantic overripe dill pickle.

The cloud came so fast and the storm was over so soon, it was no wonder no one had an exact idea of what really happened. It all happened so quickly. There was a terrific gust of wind, which whipped the dust and leaves up into a froth . . . a crashing splatter of raindrops as big as saucers, which flattened the leaves and dust back to earth . . . and it was over! And the sun came out again and the sky was clear, blue and serene as if nothing had happened.

People blinked and looked at each other and wondered if anything really had happened or if they had dreamed it. And it was strange, too, aside from stripping the leaves (that were already dead and ready to fall anyway) from some trees, and lifting a few loose barn doors from their hinges, nothing was damaged by the storm. There had been no explanation afterward or forecast before of that storm by any of the local or government weathermen. It was never recorded officially. The barometer and the thermometer did not register any change before, during or after the storm. It was all so fast.

And no one really ever knew much about that storm and about that amazing black cloud except Eddie Blow. He found out about it after supper that night.

When Eddie returned from his errand he found his grandmother shooing chickens out of her truck garden with her apron.

"Eddie boy," she called as he came up the road. "My, my! Am I glad to see you. I was worried about you. Thought you got caught in that storm. Here, help me shoo these chickens out of the tomatoes. The storm blew them over the fence. Shoo, chickens . . . out you go . . ."

In a few minutes the chickens were back in the barnyard where they belonged.

"Dear me, wasn't that the strangest thing?" said Eddie's grandmother. "Well, now is the time for the sudden blow, but never have I seen the likes of that one."

"That's what Captain Jack said," said Eddie.

"Dear me, yes. Hurry and get washed, Eddie," said his grandmother. "My biscuits ought to be done now. We'll be having supper in a minute."

And it was during supper that Eddie's grandmother asked the question which Eddie, for the past two weeks, had feared she would ask. She asked it right after they had been discussing whether to send Eddie's package back to New York by Parcel Post or Railway Express. Eddie had packed his clothes and some specimens (some rocks, curious pieces of wood and empty birds' eggs) in a cardboard carton the way he always did at the end of the summer. And, as it always happened, Grandma discussed whether they ought to send the package by Parcel Post or Railway Express.

This year Eddie favored Parcel Post because of the birds' eggshells in the package.

His grandmother was inclined toward Railway Express.

"But I guess you're right about Parcel Post," she finally admitted. "You'll be needing some of the clothes, the sweater especially, in that package when school starts. Maybe even the first day with the changeable weather we've been having. And everyone says Parcel Post is quicker than the Railway Express even though it's more expensive. And speaking of school, Eddie, what grade are you going into this year?"

"I'll be in the eighth at Junior High," said Eddie after he swallowed a big bite of blueberry pie.

"Dear me. Dear me. Seems just like yesterday when you entered the seventh in Junior High," sighed his grandmother. "Time sure does fly."

Eddie nodded and dug his fork into his pie again but the oozy purple chunk of pie slipped off his fork when his grandmother asked the question that he dreaded.

"Eddie, there's something I wanted to ask you for some time but I'm always forgetting. . . . Eddie, what grade of school is your friend Marty in?"

That was it! That was the question! Eddie stammered a little and swallowed hard.

"He looks like such a smart little boy," continued Eddie's grandmother thoughtfully. "I wondered about him. He doesn't talk much but he seems to know so much. Did you ever ask him about his school?"

"No, ma'am!" said Eddie with a sigh of relief.

There! The question had been asked and he had answered it truthfully! He never had asked Marty about his life on Martinea. And the little man had never volunteered any information about himself, his family, or anything else other than some of the scientific things he sometimes talked about.

Ever since the Boy Scout Jamboree Eddie had seen a lot of the little man. Since it was Eddie's last week at the farm before he went down to New York to go back to school, his grandmother said, as she always did at the end of the summer, that he need not do any more chores. That he could do as he pleased. And aside from an occasional errand or two to the village, Eddie lived the life of a carefree vacationer all day long.

He took the little man fishing for bullheads.

They went hiking and exploring the countryside and they talked away the fine sunny afternoons.

Fishing with the little man was a curious experience.

Eddie rigged up a couple of fishing poles, got some bait and they both sat on the bank of the brook at one of the places which Eddie knew about where, if you sat long enough, you were bound to pull in a bullhead or two. The first time they went fishing together, the little man sat silently holding his pole for a short time.

"What object sitting here?" he asked after a while.

"We're fishing for bullheads," whispered Eddie. "Don't talk loud."

"Bullheads?" whispered the little man back to Eddie. He dug out his dictionary box, flipped through it and asked, "Bullheads is animals?"

"No! Bullheads is—are fish," whispered Eddie. "Shush. . . . There's a couple of them! Keep your pole still . . . . We'll catch them sure!"

The little man peered down into the water.

"Oh . . . catch fish!" he said brightly as if

for the first time he understood what he was doing there, holding a pole with a string and a hooked worm tied to the end of it.

Then he dropped his pole and as quick as a dart slipped his hands into the brook and brought them out again in a flash, holding the squirming dripping fish.

"Catch fish!" he said triumphantly as he threw them on the bank at Eddie's feet.

Eddie blinked.

"You're supposed to catch the fish on your hook," said Eddie when he got over his surprise.

The little man shrugged his shoulders and returned to his fishing. He picked up his fishing pole again and sat there looking down into the water as silent and as rigid as a rock.

After a while a big bullhead came along, stuck his wise old head out from between some reeds in the limpid waters and rolled his eyes up at the two hooked worms that dangled temptingly in front of his blunt nose. Then he turned tail and would have swum off to a safe, peaceful old age if the little man had not suddenly sprung into action. He crouched at the edge of the brook, holding his fishing pole with one hand, then—swish! His free hand had cut into the water and out again. The big bullhead was clutched fast in his fist! He speared the finny tail of his fish onto his fishhook and turned to Eddie as proud as a peacock.

"Catch fish on hook!" he said.

And that was all the fish they caught on that first expedition. Eddie did not try to explain about fishing to the little man again that day.

Similar things happened when they went hiking together. Eddie said since the little man could not explore America with his powerless space ship he could do at least a little exploring by hiking. So Eddie planned hikes to points of interest near his grandmother's farm. They packed their knapsacks and hiked cross-country to Washington Rock, Indian Cave and Dutchman's Gulch.

On the afternoon they started for Washington Rock, Eddie pointed out the famous rock from his grandmother's front porch. He explained who George Washington, the father of our country, was. Then he told the little man the history of the rock, that it was said Washington once stood there on the rock (or rather sat on his horse who stood on the rock), that the mark of the horse's hoof is still clearly marked on its surface and that Washington looked down over the Hudson River Valley for some reason that is now lost in antiquity.

Eddie knew there were many Washington Rocks around, almost as many rocks that Washington stood on as there were beds he slept in. Eddie had hiked to one in New Jersey with his New York Scout troop and to another in Connecticut. But this local Washington Rock was special because it was the only one which showed the mark of George Washington's horse's hoof.

The little man listened to the end of the story, and when Eddie finished he pointed to the rock resting on its distant hill and he asked, "Now walk to this rock?"

And as Eddie nodded, the little man started walking in a straight line toward Washington Rock. Nothing stopped him! He walked, as the crow flies, in a straight line for the Washington Rock. He did not walk around anything but marched ahead in a straight line up the side of anything that stood in his way, over the top of it and down the other side.

That's the way he traveled over big field boulders, steep cliffs, old sheds, hay mounds and every obstacle he encountered. And even though the knobs on his non-gravity shoes were set to zero, the non-gravity power of his shoes was working.

Eddie was soon exhausted trying to keep up with him because Eddie had to walk around things. The next time they went hiking, Eddie did not point out to the little man where they were going. And the little man did not know where they were going until they got there. Eddie found hiking that way less tiring and a lot more fun.

On the one rainy day during the past week, Eddie with his raincoat on and with the permission of his grandmother, went visiting the little man. He found him polishing his gadgets. They sat around in the cozy yellow glow of the old stable lantern that Eddie had given the little man to light the space ship and talked about a lot of things. But nothing was said about school or things like that. Eddie really did not know anything about Marty's life on Martinea. The little man asked Eddie a lot of questions about himself but he never answered anything Eddie asked him. Maybe he had a reason.

But now, as Eddie was finishing his supper

with a second piece of blueberry pie, he thought and worried about the little man's future. What would happen to him when Eddie went away? What would happen when the men started to pick and pack the apples as they did every fall after Eddie went back to school? The apples were beginning to get big and red already. What would happen when the men went up to the orchard and found Marty and his space ship hidden away in the gully in back of Grandfather's apple tree? Or if he could keep himself and the Astral Rocket Disk hidden and they did not find him, if the little man could not get back to his home in Martinea, how could he possibly live through the winter in the space ship? The winters were very cold out in the country, and the Astral Rocket Disk had no heating equipment that Eddie remembered seeing.

Eddie thought he might suggest to his grandmother that she take the little man in. She could adopt him sort of. She liked Marty and she always said it was lonesome on the farm in the wintertime. Of course, the little man could work for his keep, do some chores, feed the stock. . . .

As Eddie tried to figure out some way of

bringing the subject up, sounds of heavy feet were heard out on the front porch.

"That must be Marty," said Eddie's grandmother with a smile. "I can recognize the sound of his heavy shoes any time. . . . Marty!" she called, "is that you? Come in, boy. We're here in the kitchen. Come in and have a piece of fresh blueberry pie."

They heard his heavy shoes march down the hall, and in another moment the little man stood in the kitchen.

"My! . . . My! . . . My! . . . Marty!" cried Eddie's grandmother. "Really, Marty. You're all spruced up."

The little man stood there, grinning from ear to ear. He was dressed, not in the tattered old jeans and Cub Scout shirt that he had worn since Eddie lent them to him, but he wore his own neat dark-green suit, both the trousers and the jacket. His buttons had been scrubbed until they glistened. His suit had been brushed until it looked like any good suit looks like when it is carefully and completely brushed. Even his big non-gravity shoes had been polished.

He held a neatly folded bundle under his arm. The bundle was Eddie's jeans and the

Cub Scout shirt. He put the neat bundle on the table.

"Aren't you the dandy, though?" laughed Eddie's grandmother. "You are absolutely spick and span. I'd be honored to have so polished a little gentleman eat a big piece of my blueberry pie in my kitchen. Sit down, Marty."

The little man smiled proudly and made a little gesture with his hand, palm out, that thanked Eddie's grandmother but refused the pie.

"No time," he said. "Must say good-bye!"

Then he stuck his hand toward Eddie's grandmother.

"Well, Marty, I'm real sorry to see you go," she said, as she shook his outthrust hand in both of hers. "Come see us again sometime. . . . Good-bye, Marty."

When she turned to pick up a plate from the table the little man caught Eddie's eye and jerked his head toward the door. Then he turned on his heel and walked out to the porch. Eddie ran after him.

10. MESSAGE FROM MARTINEA

"What's happened, Marty?" asked Eddie in an excited whisper. "How come? What happened?"

The little man looked quickly at one of the peculiar dials on the bracelet that served him as a watch.

"Must return to Martinea. Time for take-off tonight. Three hours before morning begin." He spoke briskly. "No time to talk."

Eddie figured quickly in his head.

"You mean three hours before midnight? Nine o'clock? Oh, you've got plenty of time.

Come on, tell me what happened. Begin telling me quick."

The little man knit his brows, took a deep breath and began.

"Today on three o'clock, United States Daylight Saving Time, receive message direct from Martinea."

"WHAT!" Eddie shouted. "You received a message from—"

"Keep voice down!" ordered the little man.

"Did you say you received a message from Martinea?" asked Eddie in a hoarse whisper. "But how? . . . What? . . . How could you?"

"Through new very important scientific power in Martinea!" said the little man happily. "Received message on Willenwingulagulin."

"On the Willenwingul . . . . Say!" whispered Eddie, "isn't that the jigger hanging in the disk you said was old-fashioned? Not modern?"

The little man nodded.

Eddie knew the little man cleaned and polished all the equipment in the Astral Rocket Disk every day, including the old-fashioned jigger, the Willenwingulagulin, which he never expected to use, even if he got a fresh supply of Zurianomatichrome Power. Eddie thought he just cleaned up everything like that because the little man was naturally tidy.

"But what did the message say?" asked Eddie. "What did the whatever-you-call-it tell you?"

The little man held up one finger for silence.

"Wait," he said, sternly. "Must talk much. I tell."

Then he went on to say that at approximately three o'clock that afternoon the old-fashioned jigger began to send out feeble signals. The little man opened its throttle as wide as it would go and he received the message.

"But what did the message say?" Eddie repeated eagerly.

The little man held up his silencing finger once more.

"Message say, stand by, will send Radar-Interspacial-Super-Power-Antimagnetic Ray to recharge Zurianomatichrome Wire. Expose wire to Super-Power-Antimagnetic Ray."

Eddie gasped!

"You mean they can send a super-special-super power to recharge your Secret Power here—all the way from Martinea?"

"Yes! Can send!" said the little man, and he paused dramatically. "Yes! Can send. . . . Did send!"

"Gosh, you mean your wire got Secret Power Z again!"

Eddie sat down on the porch step with a bang.

The little man smiled proudly and drew the spool of Zurianomatichrome Wire out of his pocket. It was so shiny it glowed in the gathering darkness like a small moon in his hand.

"Well! What d'you know. What d'you know," was all Eddie could say. Then after a moment he thought of something else. "But how did they find you, Marty? How did they know your ship was in Grandma's apple orchard?"

The little man opened his eyes wide, as if Eddie had asked a surprisingly stupid question.

"Martinean scientists use Universal-Spacial-Communication Beam. On Martinea our scientists know all time where is Martinean space ship," he said proudly.

"Oh!" said Eddie. "Excuse me. I thought . . . ," and he was about to say he thought the little man was lost or out of contact with his home base on Martinea, but the little man did not want to hear what Eddie thought. He went on with his story.

He said that in just about a fraction of a clock tick after he had received the surprise message, some great force struck the axis of the Astral Rocket Disk. And in that instant the walls of the space ship lighted up with the blue-tinged light. Instruments and gadgets, which had for the past few weeks been still, suddenly began to tick, whir and flutter. And the Zurianomatichrome Wire, which he had installed in its proper place in the column, sputtered. The Astral Rocket Disk was charged with Secret Power Z again!

"Say—" Eddie interrupted as he remembered the strange storm and the weird black cloud he had witnessed in the village that afternoon. "Say, I betcha that black cloud and that storm that came all of a sudden—"

"Which black cloud? Which storm?" asked the little man.

"It came up this afternoon. I saw it down at the general store," said Eddie quickly. "First this big black cloud, like a big soft dill pickle or something . . . well, I figure the storm might have come because the great force was sent from Martinea. I betcha that made the storm."

"No! Can no be!" said the little man stiffly. "Martinean scientists can no make mistake! Martinean scientists direct great force only to wire on Astral Rocket Disk. Great force travel direct to charge one point in complete universe. Martinean scientists make pinpoint landing. No mistake."

"But there was a storm," insisted Eddie. "Maybe the great force sort of spread a little."

"No! Can no be!" said the little man. Then he shrugged his shoulders and admitted the great force might have caused "possible little disturbance in earth's atmosphere."

And he dismissed the storm with that shrug of his shoulders. But Eddie was pretty sure the black cloud and the flash storm must have been caused by that charge of super-special Secret Power recharging the Astral Rocket Disk. Eddie had read about such clouds forming at atomic explosions. Well, naturally, something similar ought to happen when a force like atomic power or superior to atomic power.

. . . Eddie stopped thinking about these scientific things because he was getting a little mixed up and he listened to the little man again.

"After Great Force charged disk, I received message number two. It say, return Martinea at once," said the little man. "Now I must return to Martinea tonight. Nine o'clock."

"Say, that's great!" said Eddie enthusiastically. "Gosh, that's swell. I'm sure happy everything worked out. I'm happy for you, I mean, that you can get back to Martinea."

The little man shook his head. He did not look happy now that he finished talking.

"What's the matter? Don't you wanna go back to Martinea?" asked Eddie.

"Yes, want to go back," said the little man.

"So what's the matter?" asked Eddie.

"I must return Martinea," said the little man sadly. "No finish mission to explore United States of America."

"Aw, that's too bad," said Eddie sympathetically.

They were both silent for a moment. The little man heaved a deep sigh.

"Now I must tell truth," he said in a low voice. "Like Boy Scout, must tell truth."

"What d'you mean, Marty?" asked Eddie. "What truth, Marty?"

The little man drew himself up, straightened his shoulders and looked Eddie square in the eyes.

"Yes . . . must tell truth. . . . I no Scientist Explorer from planet Martinea!"

"WHAT!" exclaimed Eddie. "You're not a Scientist Explorer from Martinea?"

The little man's eyes fell. "Yes," he said with downcast eyes. "I no Scientist Explorer from Planet Martinea . . . . I only . . . Junior Scientist Explorer."

"Oh!" said Eddie.

"Now I must return to Martinea. I fail my mission to explore America," continued the little man sadly. "Now I never become full Scientist Explorer."

"Gosh," said Eddie quietly. "Gosh, that's too bad."

Eddie sat and thought awhile.

"Say, lookit here," he said. "I never asked you about yourself or about Martinea. But here's something I gotta know. What were you sent here for? . . . I mean, to explore America? Does Martinea want to conquer America? Make war or something like that? What you gotta explore America for?"

The little man stepped back with a shocked expression on his face. He hunted through his dictionary box which he had not used much for the past week (Eddie and he had understood each other) until he found the words he wanted.

"Martinea no conquer! Martinea no interest in war!" he said sincerely. "Martinea interest in United States of America pure scientific interest." And he hunted through his dictionary box for a special word. "Curiosity!" he said finally. "Yes, Martinea interest in United States of America pure scientific curiosity!"

"Oh!" said Eddie, and he sat and thought another minute.

"You know what! . . . Guess I can help. . . . Wait here a minute."

Eddie ran into the house and in a few minutes he was out again. He carried something in his arms.

"Lookit here," he said. "If you went around exploring the United States what would you find? You'd find out about the people. What they do. Where they live and things like that."

The little man nodded.

"And you'd find out more things, like what they raise and what they manufacture and things like that. . . . Huh?"

Again the little man nodded.

"Then maybe you'd find out something about the lakes and the rivers and the mountains. And you'd find out about the government and the laws and things like that."

The little man nodded for the third time.

"Well, here are these books. I asked Grandma if I could give them to you and she said I could. Here's my fifth-year geography book and here's my last year's history book. I've got them here because I hadda catch up on some things this summer. I was out of school with measles once. Now these books'll tell you about us Americans. That history book has the Declaration of Independence in it and Lincoln's Gettysburg speech. You can take them back to Martinea with you."

The little man was overwhelmed as he took the books which Eddie thrust at him.

"And here's another one," said Eddie quietly. "It's my new Boy Scout *Manual*. I'll save up and get another one when I go back to New York. Betcha, if you study those books on your way back, you'll know more about America than anybody in Martinea. And you can have this, too, if you want it."

Eddie piled a folded something on the books the little man held in his arms. It was Eddie's old folded up Cub Scout shirt.

For a moment they both were too embarrassed to say a thing. Suddenly the little man rested the bundle of books on the porch, turned his back and fussed around with something out of one of his pockets. He worked furiously for a few minutes, then he turned and gave Eddie two shiny small objects.

"This for her," he said, holding out a twisted wire ring as he pointed into the house. Then he held out the other object. "This for you."

His present for Eddie was a Boy Scout badge. He had just made it as he stood there. Both the badge and the ring were made from his precious shiny Zurianomatichrome Wire!

Then the little man gathered up the books and the Cub Scout shirt and put out his hand to Eddie. They shook hands like Boy Scouts shake hands.

"Good-bye . . . Friend," said the little man.

And he bent down quickly, twirled the knob on his non-gravity shoes to the sixty-mile-speed-limit mark and left the porch in a flash.

Eddie sat on the porch alone in the darkness. After a while when his grandmother had finished the dishes she came out and sat on her rocker.

"What you sitting in the dark for, Eddie?" she asked. "Here, I'll turn on the porch light. There are no mosquitoes around tonight. It's nice reading the paper out here . . . a little chilly, but nice."

Eddie did not say anything. He just sat there thinking.

"Oh, Eddie," said his grandmother, "is Marty gone?"

"Yes, Grandma," said Eddie. "He left this with me to give you."

Eddie reached over and dropped the shiny wire ring in his grandmother's outstretched hand.

"Oh, that is nice. . . . It's a ring, isn't it?" she said. "How pretty and shiny. Yes, Marty's a nice boy. Hope we see him again sometime."

"Hope so," said Eddie.

After another spell of silence his grandmother looked up from her newspaper and spoke again.

"I see by the paper that we ought to be seeing some Northern Lights tonight. Watch for them, Eddie. It's sort of early in the year to be seeing Northern Lights but I hope we see them."

Eddie nodded and looked out at the sky over the ridge for a time.

"There they are, Grandma," said Eddie, as the long mysterious fingers of the Northern Lights began to weave across the sky. "Grandma, the Northern Lights are beginning to show."

"So they are, Eddie. Northern Lights are so pretty," said Eddie's grandmother. "Somehow they make me think . . . well, like as if I was seeing the sound of music, good rich-sounding music from an orchestra or an organ."

They watched the lights flowing, wavering and dying away into the darkness. And suddenly, just as the porcelain clock in the parlor struck nine, a long beam of light sprang up from the ridge in back of Grandfather's apple tree, and in an instant it shot straight up across the sky and was gone.

Eddie reached up his arms to wave because

he thought he knew who rode that beam of light. But he felt his grandmother's eyes on his back . . . so he changed his gesture to a stretch and pretended to yawn.

"Eddie boy, you're stretching and yawning," said his grandmother gently. "It's nine o'clock. You'd better be getting ready for bed, son."

Next morning Eddie walked up to the apple orchard. He stood on the ridge back of Grandfather's apple tree and looked down at the spot where the space ship had been. There was no sign of the gully. It had been filled up and covered neatly with old twigs and branches. In the center of the refilled gully stood the old stable lantern Eddie had loaned his friend Marty to light his space ship.